Even Firefighters HUG Their Moms

Christine Kole MacLean · *Illustrated by* **Mike Reed**

PUFFIN BOOKS

PUFFIN BOOKS
Published by Penguin Group
Penguin Young Readers Group,
345 Hudson Street, New York, New York 10014, U.S.A.
Penguin Books Ltd, 80 Strand, London WC2R ORL, England
Penguin Books Australia Ltd, 250 Camberwell Road,
Camberwell, Victoria 3124, Australia
Penguin Books Canada Ltd, 10 Alcorn Avenue, Toronto,
Ontario, Canada M4V 3B2
Penguin Books (N.Z.) Ltd, 182-190 Wairau Road,
Auckland 10, New Zealand

First published in the United States of America by Dutton Children's Books,
a division of Penguin Putnam Books for Young Readers, 2002
Published by Puffin Books, a division of Penguin Young Readers Group, 2004

13 15 17 19 20 18 16 14

THE LIBRARY OF CONGRESS HAS CATALOGED THE DUTTON EDITION AS FOLLOWS:
MacLean, Christine Kole.
Even firefighters hug their moms / by Christine Kole MacLean;
illustrated by Mike Reed.
p. cm.
Summary: An imaginative boy pretends to be a firefighter, policeman,
construction worker, and other busy people, but he realizes that it is
important to take time to give his mom a hug.
ISBN: 0-525-46996-6 (hc)
[1. Occupations—Fiction. 2. Imagination—Fiction.
3. Mother and child—Fiction.]
I. Reed, Mike, 1951– ill. II. Title.
PZ7.M22423 Ev 2002   [E]—dc21   2002004449

Puffin Books ISBN 978-0-142-40191-0

Manufactured in China

To Clark and Madeline,
who daily take me places
I never could have imagined
—C.K.M.

To Jane, Alex, and Joe
—M.R.

My name is Big Frank, and I'm a firefighter. Every morning I get up and look at the newspaper to find out where the fires are. Then I get dressed in my protective gear.

My air tank and face mask help me breathe even if the smoke is as thick as a milk shake.

I climb onto my hook and ladder truck and drive to the fire. Sometimes Firefighter Sally comes with me.

When we get to the fire, we rush into the burning building.

"How about a hug?" my mom asks as I run by.

"Too busy fighting fires," I say.

"Even firefighters hug their moms," she says.

My name is Officer Dave, and this is Rex, my police dog.

We stand guard at the door and when criminals come by, I announce it on the loudspeaker to warn everyone. "Stand back!" I say. "Criminals coming through."

Then we lock up all the criminals in jail. My mom walks by. "Don't worry about your safety, ma'am," I say. "We've got you covered."

"How about covering me with a hug?" she asks.

"No time," I say. "We've got to serve and protect."

"Even police officers hug their moms," she says.

My name is Joe, and I'm an EMT. That's short for "emergency medical technician." My partner, Junior, is in training. I'm teaching her everything I know.

Over the radio we hear about an accident, and we spring into action. We bandage up the man's cuts and scrapes and put him on a stretcher. We give him a bowl of ice cream to make him feel better.

Then we race to the hospital. We keep the siren on the whole way. *WEE-ooo, WEE-ooo, WEE-ooo!*

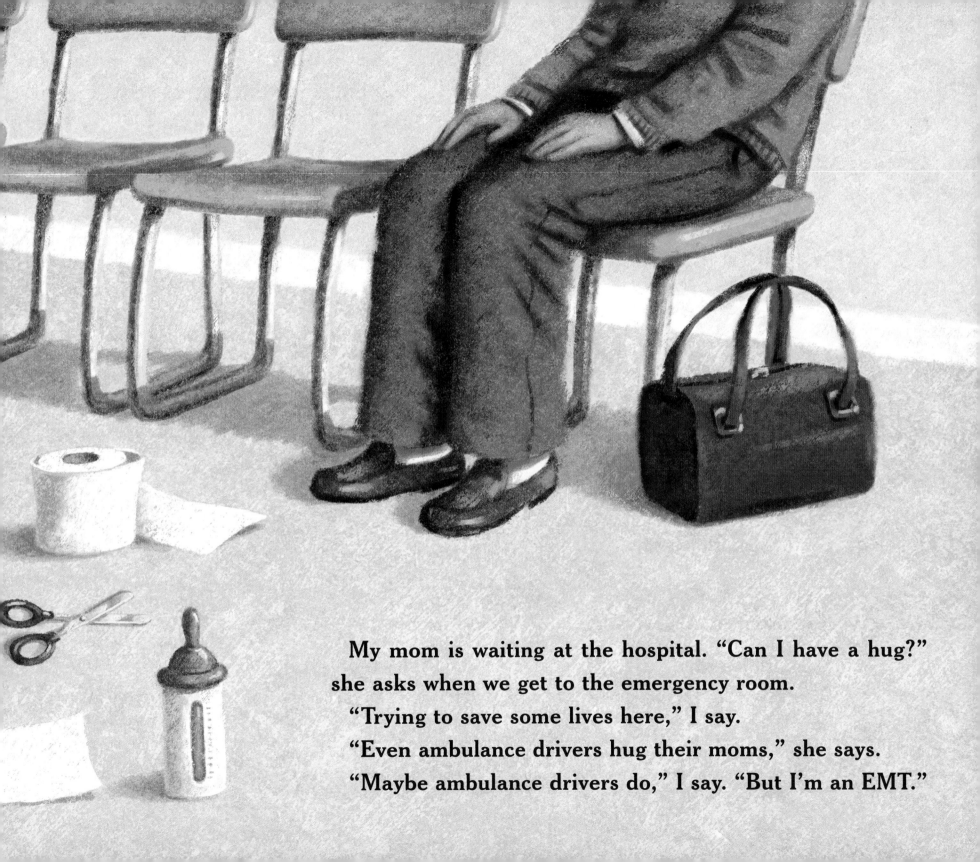

My mom is waiting at the hospital. "Can I have a hug?" she asks when we get to the emergency room.

"Trying to save some lives here," I say.

"Even ambulance drivers hug their moms," she says.

"Maybe ambulance drivers do," I say. "But I'm an EMT."

My name is Dan, and I'm a construction worker.

I drive a front loader. I make the yellow light flash. When I back up, the *BEEP! BEEP! BEEP!* tells everyone to get out of the way.

Sometimes people watch me work. They ask if they can help. I say thanks, but no. Better leave the heavy work to the pros.

"Can you take a coffee break and give me a hug?" my mom shouts.

"Coffee break's over," I shout back.

"Even construction workers hug their moms," she says.

I'm Captain Steve, and I'm a helicopter pilot. I work for the Coast Guard. I rescue people from their boats during hurricanes and tornadoes and other gigantic storms. My partner uses a winch to pull them to safety.

"Can I hug the hero?" my mom asks.

I shake my head. "It's just part of the job," I say.
"Even helicopter pilots hug their moms," she says.
Whop-whop-whop-whop-whop-whop-whop, go the blades.
"Sorry! I can't hear you!" I yell, pointing up at the blades.

My name is Sam, and I'm the conductor of this train.
"Tickets, please!" I call to the people waiting to get on.
I take their tickets as they board.
One of them tries to sneak a pig onboard.
"No farm animals!" I say. "This is a *passenger* train."

"What do you get when you buy a ticket?" a lady asks.

"You get a ride to Chicago," I say.

"Snacks?"

"No, but you can buy food in the dining car."

"Hugs?"

"No, no hugs. Only a ride to Chicago."

"Even conductors hug their moms," she says.

WOO-WOOOOO! goes the whistle.

"All aboard!" I say. "This train is leaving the station."

My name is Neil, and I'm an astronaut. This is my rocket. Yesterday I went to the moon. Don't believe anyone who tries to tell you it's made of cheese. It's made out of rock. Trust me.

Today I'm going to Mars. I radio Mission Control. When they give me the thumbs-up, I blast off.

"What's Mars made of?" my mom asks.

I tell her Legos.

"I'm surprised you came back," she says.

"I'm here to get my Lego men, then I'm going back again," I say.

"Any chance you'll give me a hug first?" she asks.

"No," I say.

"Wait just a minute, Buster," she says. "I gave you directions to Mars. A quick hug doesn't seem like too much to ask."

I shrug. "Well, it's a little hard to hug when you're wearing a bulky space suit."

"Huh," she says. "Even astronauts hug their moms."

My name is Rick, and I'm a garbage-truck driver.

I stop at each house and pick up trash, like worn-out toasters, slimy food wrappers, and pacifiers that are bad for the baby's teeth.

I turn on the crusher. It mashes everything down so more trash will fit. It goes *Clunk! Whirrrr! Creeeee!*

Whenever a lady throws something out by mistake, I get it back for her.

Sometimes the lady is so happy that she tries to give me a hug. I let her, because...

...even garbage-truck drivers hug their moms.

Sometimes.